VOYAGE

For Alexander—B.C.

For Tim, from now until the end of time may

you sail with gentle wind—K.R.

A portion of the royalties for
this book will benefit the Center
for the Book in the
Library of Congress.

www.bunkerhillpublishing.com

Bunker Hill Publishing, Inc.

285 River Road, Piermont
New Hampshire 03779, USA

10 9 8 7 6 5 4 3 2 1

Text copyright Billy Collins 2014
Illustration copyright Karen Romagna 2014

Library of Congress Control Number 2014933761
ISBN 978-1-59373-154-0
e-book ISBN 978-1-59373-177-9

Designed by JDL
Printed in China

VOYAGE

by Billy Collins

illustrated by Karen Romagna

A boy climbs into a boat

and pushes off to the open sea

and when he loses sight of land,

the boat becomes a book

which the boy begins to read

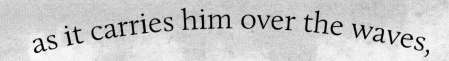

as it carries him over the waves,

and when he has finished reading,

the boy becomes the book,

and the wind from an
illustration in that book, blown

from the mouth of a cloud
with puffed-up cheeks,

as well as a rising moon drawn
at the top of the page

which looks down with such

loving amusement

on the night sea,

on the boat, the book, and the boy.

VOYAGE

A boy climbs into a boat
and pushes off to the open sea
and when he loses sight of land,
the boat becomes a book
which the boy begins to read
as it carries him over the waves,
and when he has finished reading,
the boy becomes the book,

and the wind from an
illustration in that book, blown
from the mouth of a cloud
with puffed-up cheeks,
as well as a rising moon drawn
at the top of the page
which looks down with such
loving amusement
on the night sea, on the boa
the book, and the boy